A BEASTY STORY

for Lyla

from

Steve Kellogg

A BEASTY STORY

HUFF
PUFF
HUFF
PUFF
HUFF
PUFF
HUFF
PUFF
HUFF
PUFF

NICK
5

HANK
6

SNIPPETY
SNICK
SNIPPETY
SNICK
SNIPPETY
SNICK

Bill Martin Jr & Steven Kellogg

VOYAGER BOOKS · HARCOURT, INC.

San Diego   New York   London

First Voyager Books edition 2002
Voyager Books is a trademark of Harcourt, Inc., registered in the United States of America and/or other jurisdictions.
The Library of Congress has cataloged the hardcover edition as follows: Martin, Bill, 1916– A beasty story/by
Bill Martin Jr and Steven Kellogg; illustrated by Steven Kellogg.   p. cm.
Summary: A group of mice venture into a dark, dark wood where they find a dark brown house with a dark red stair leading past
other dark colors to a spooky surprise.
[1. Mice—Fiction. 2. Color—Fiction. 3. Stories in rhyme.] I. Kellogg, Steven, ill. II. Title.
PZ8.3.M3988Be 1999 [E]—dc21   97-49519   ISBN 0-15-201683-X   ISBN 0-15-216560-6 pb

LEO 10 9 8 7 6
4500238854

This way to the dark DARK WOOD

Don't go.

With love and appreciation
to Michael Sampson and his family
—B. M. & S. K.

In a dark, dark wood there is a dark, dark house.

In the dark brown house
there is a dark, dark stair.

there is a dark, dark cellar.

there is a dark, dark cupboard.

there is a dark, dark bottle.

the dark green bottle.

A BEAST!

It floats out of the dark green bottle,

through the dark purple cupboard,

up the dark red stair,

out of the dark brown house,

into the dark, dark night,

through the dark, dark wood,

toward an even **DARKER** house,

into a dark orange room,

and GRABS HIM!

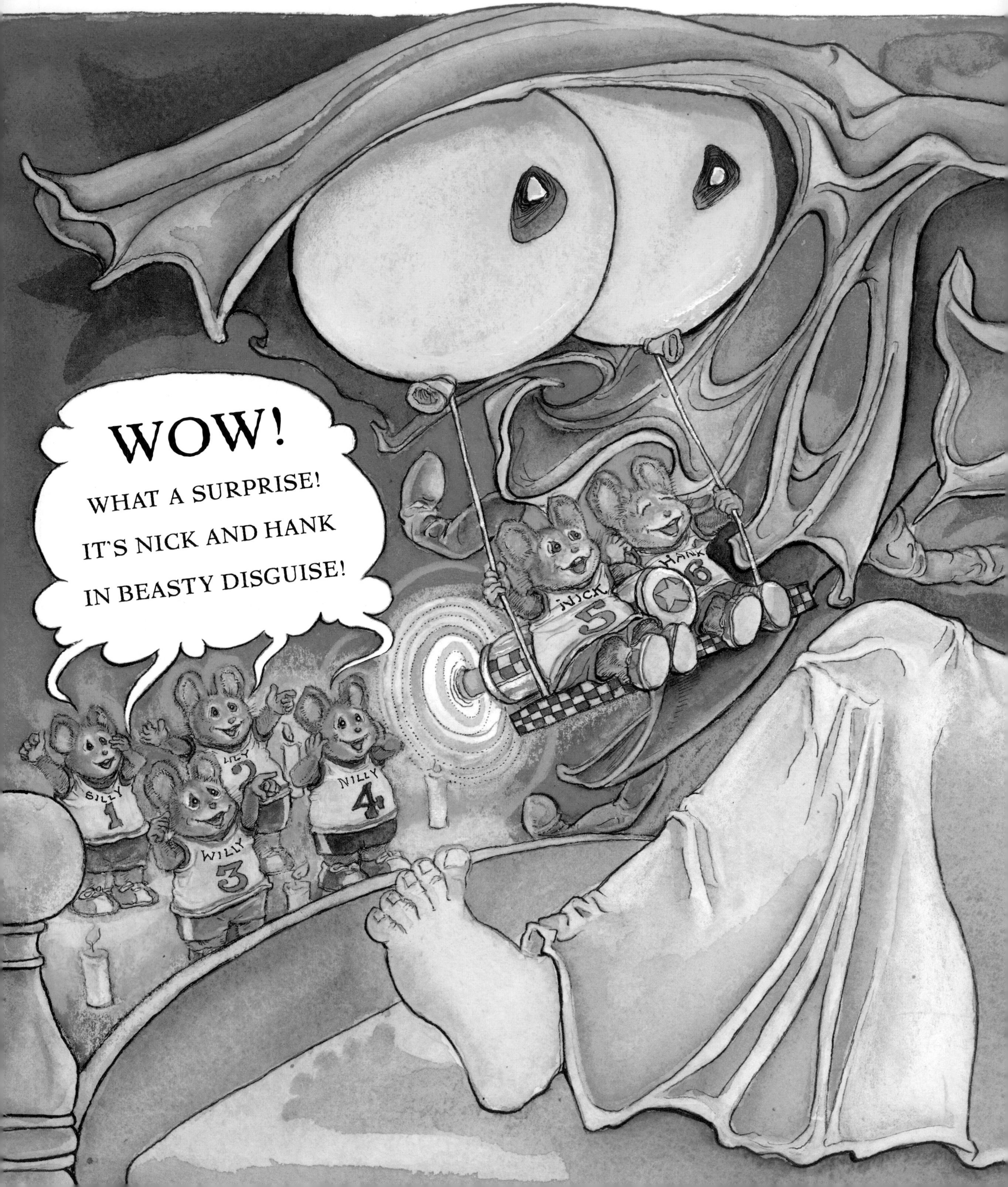

There is a flash of light!

sounds of beasty laughter,

followed by beasty snores.

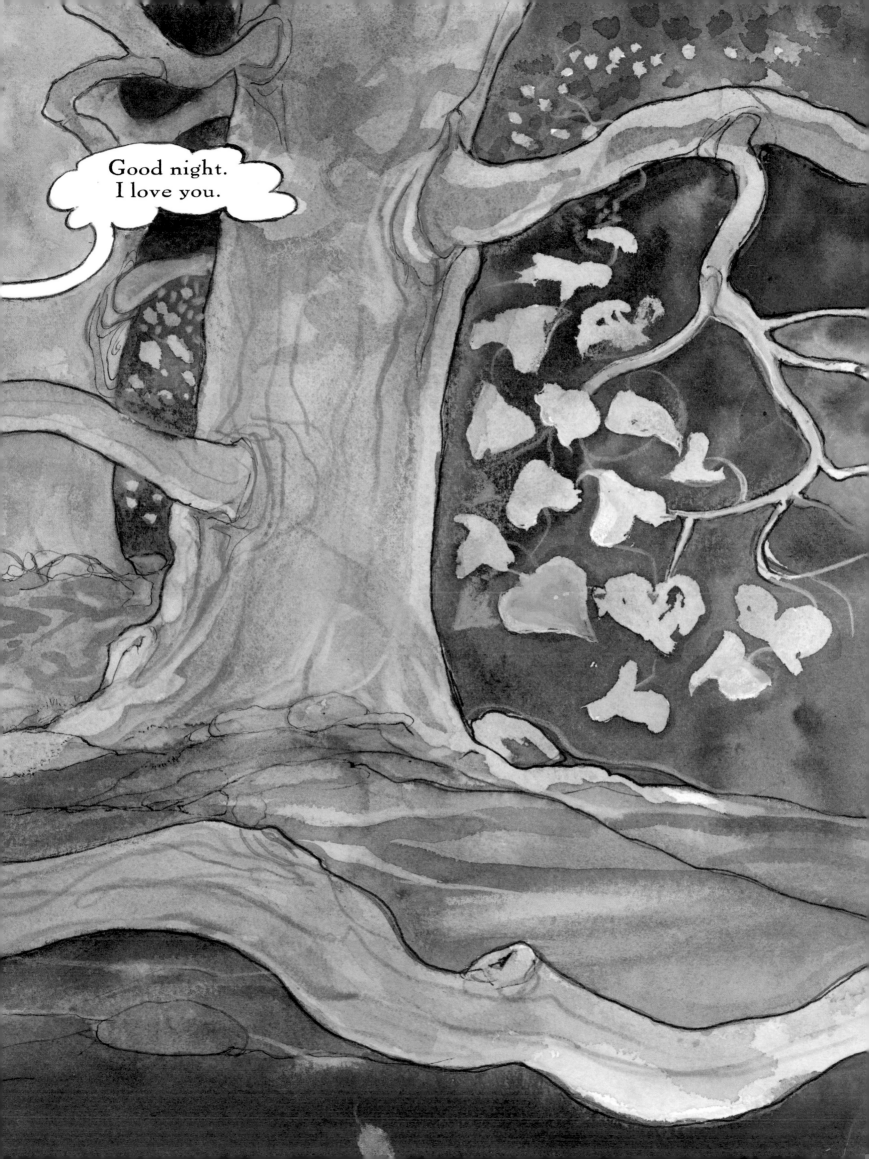

The first collaboration between two beloved creators of children's books!

BILL MARTIN JR is known worldwide for his classic picture books, including *Brown Bear, Brown Bear, What Do You See?* and *Polar Bear, Polar Bear, What Do You Hear?*, both illustrated by Eric Carle, and *Chicka Chicka Boom Boom*, illustrated by Lois Ehlert. Mr. Martin lives in Texas.

STEVEN KELLOGG has illustrated more than a hundred dearly loved books for children, including *A Hunting We Will Go!* and his own versions of the ever-popular tall tales *Johnny Appleseed*, *Pecos Bill*, and *Paul Bunyan*. Mr. Kellogg lives in Connecticut.